BABY'S
LITTLE HELPER
Coloring and Activity Book

Helping siblings to accept and understand baby's needs

About The Author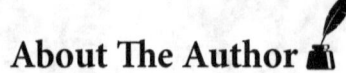

Marcia 'Cia' Harris, a proud Jamaican, was born in Linstead in the Parish of St Catherine. She currently resides in the U.S.A.

Marcia believes in empowerment: whether it be as a Life Insurance Advisor, an Early Childhood Educator or a Newborn Care Specialist, aka 'Baby Nurse' providing care to newborns, with specialization in Sleep Training or as an Emotional Support Coach to New Parents, especially moms, she gives her best.
She is a natural Story Teller, with a Diploma in Child Psychology, Special Education and Management of Early Childhood Centre. She is the Founder/Operator of YOUR DREAM BABY MANUAL; a Baby and Nanny Training and Referral Service, catering to baby and childcare needs.

She is inspired to write her children's 'DreamBook Series,' from personalized daily experiences with children as they maneuver and overcome the many hurdles faced and the resilience shown in adverse situations, including a new addition in the form of a Baby to the household. Her Inspiration also comes from stories and songs she has created for babies with whom she has worked over time.

Marcia's motto is 'Today's Children; tomorrow's future.'

A proud mom to daughter Terri-Ann and son Michael her two amazing adult children, sister, aunt, cousin and friend to many, She is happiest in the company of babies and young children.

This book is presented to

_____

By: _____

Dated: _____

Special Message: _____

_____

_____

_____

_____

How many caps are there? Count and circle the right number.

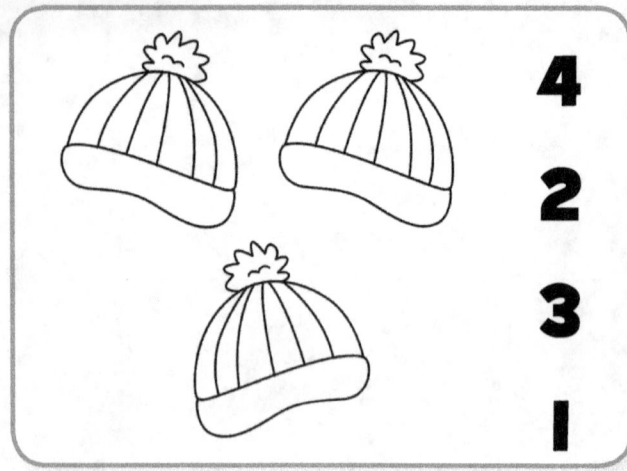

4
2
3
1

6
4
5
3

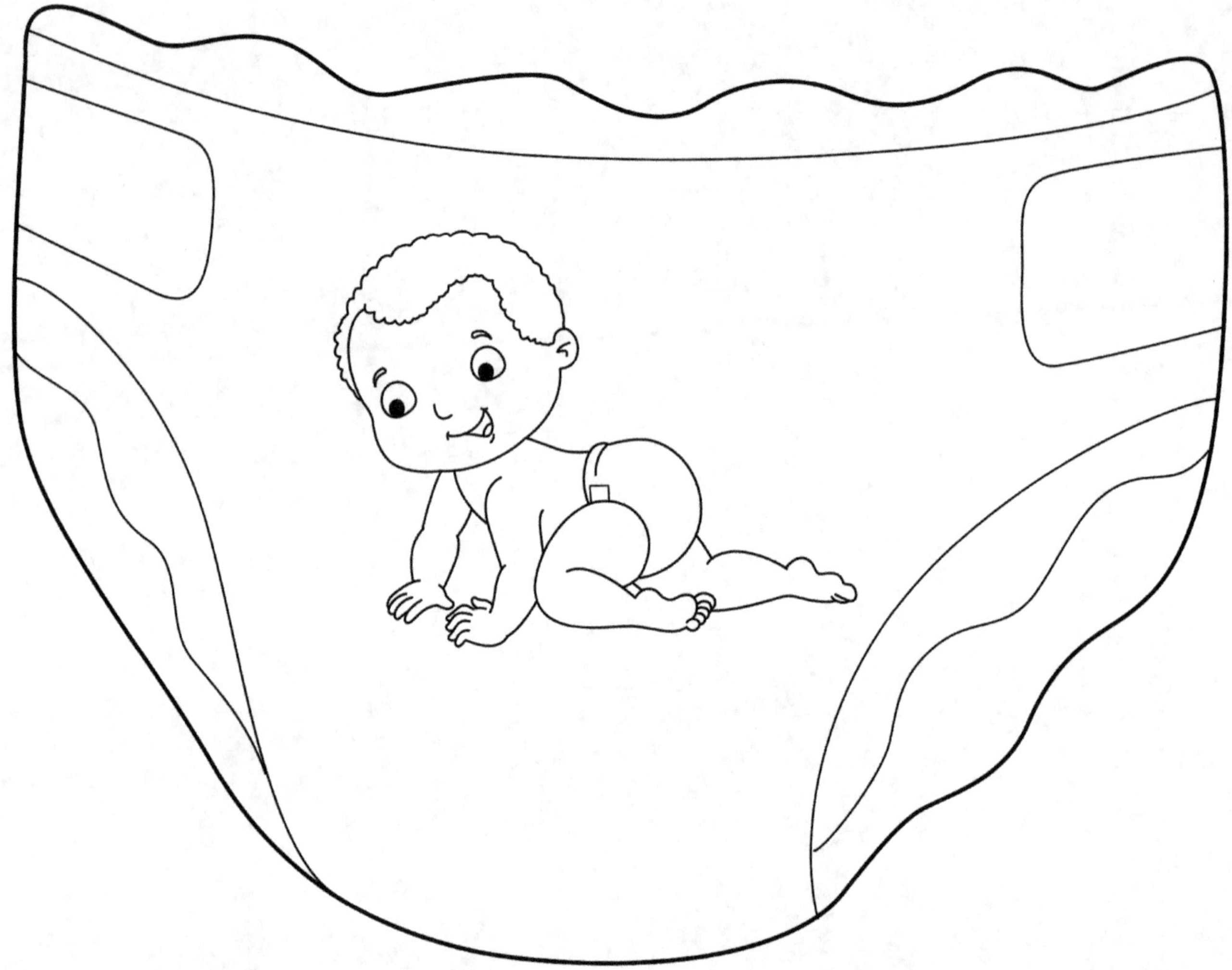

Circle the different picture.

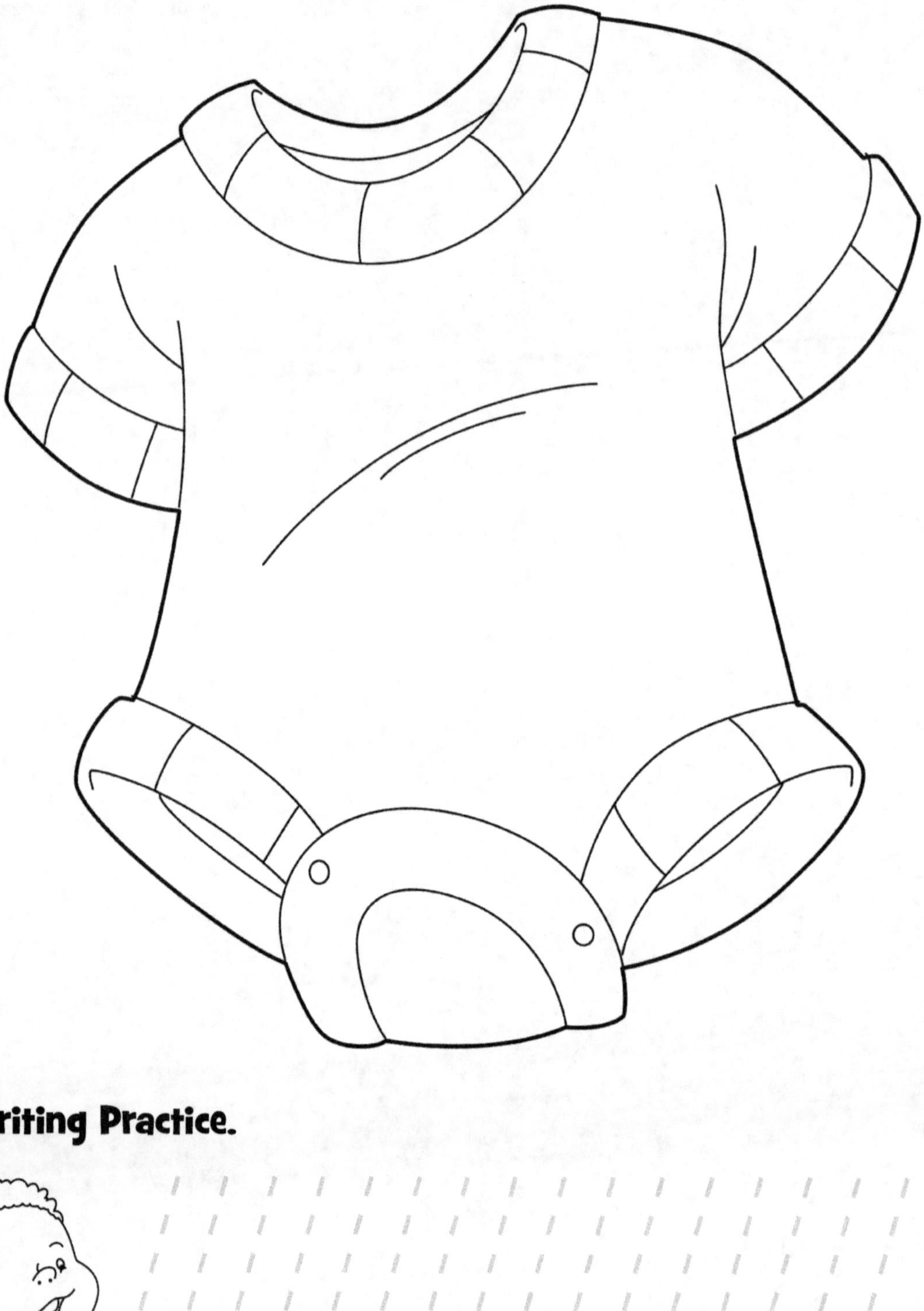

Handwriting Practice.

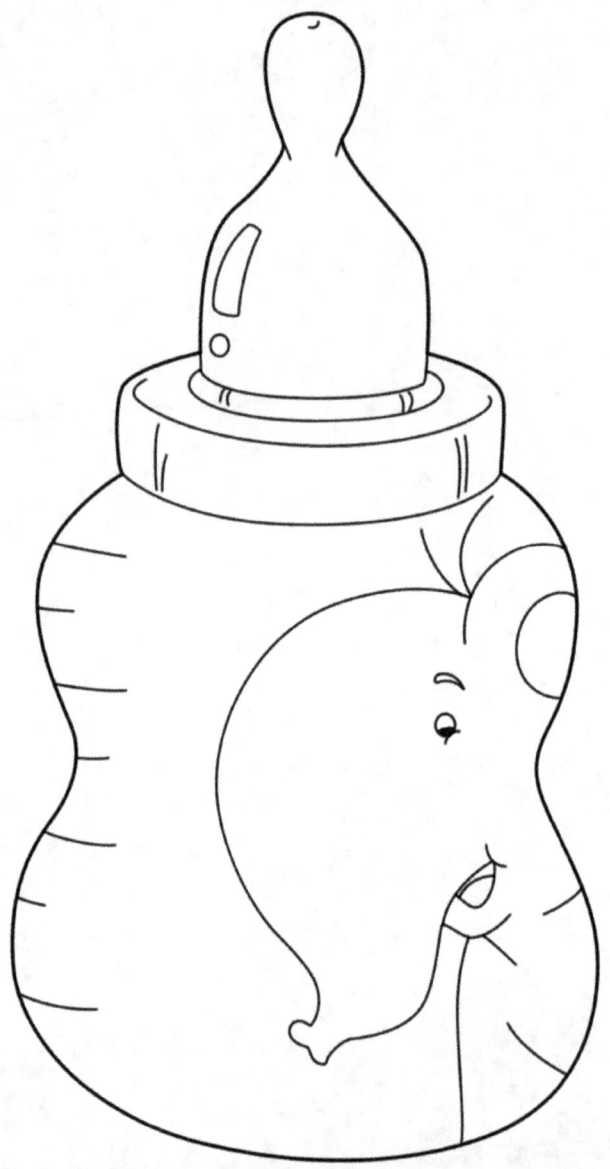

Circle the pictures that are the same.

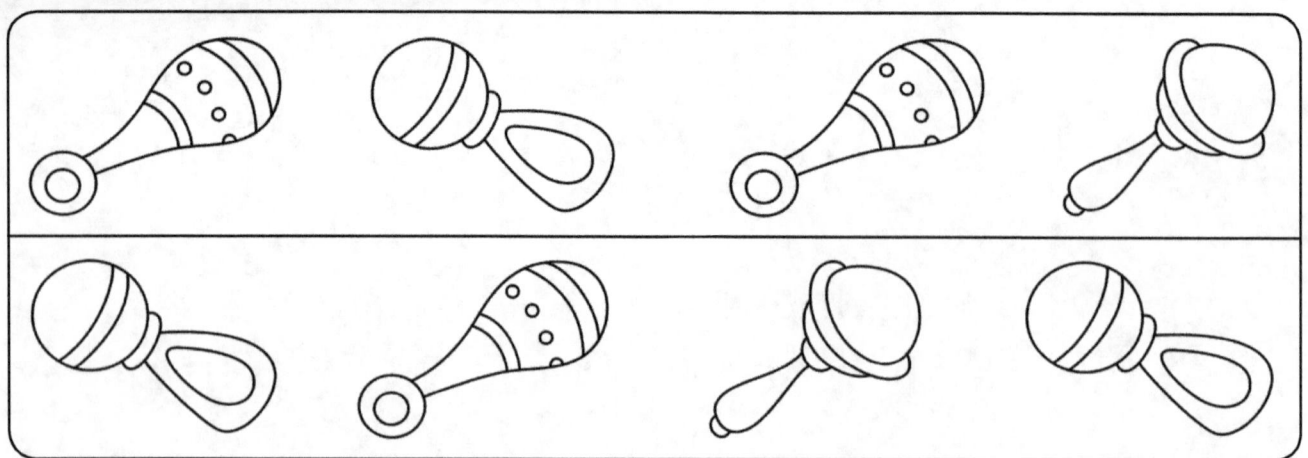

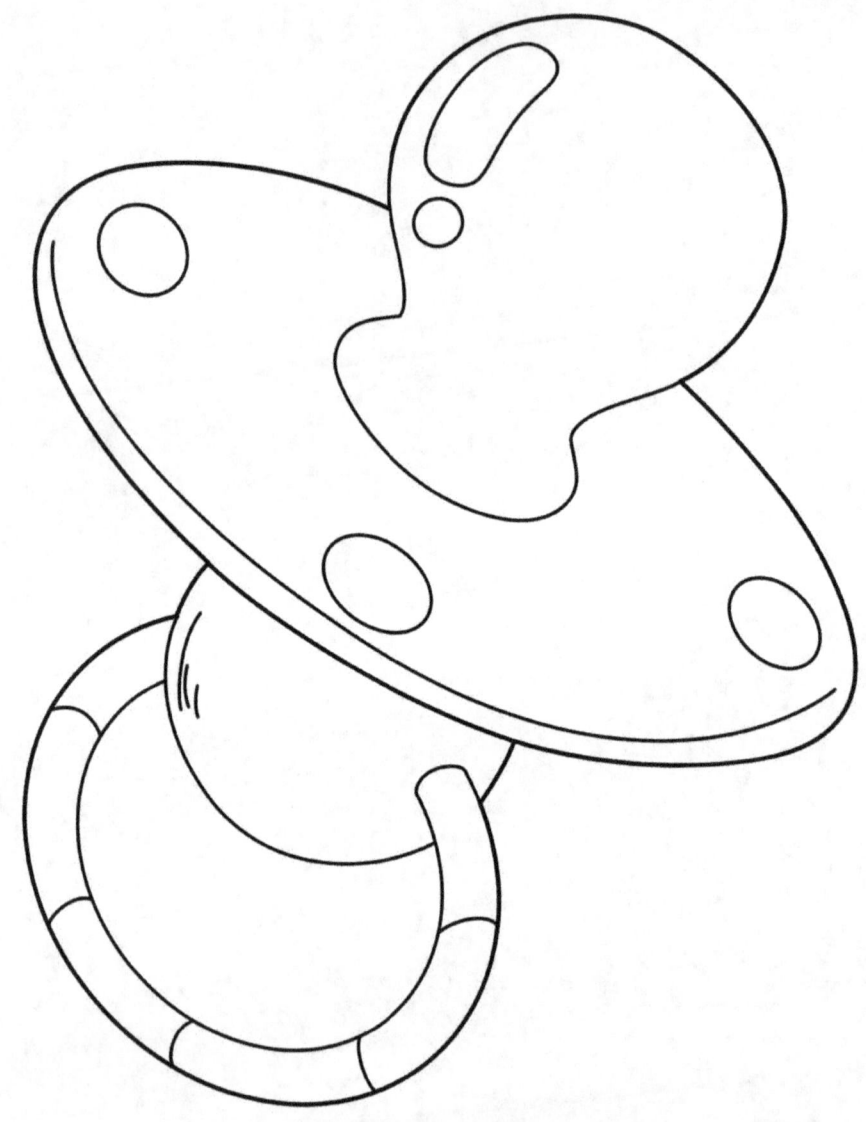

Circle the picture with name starting with the letter B.

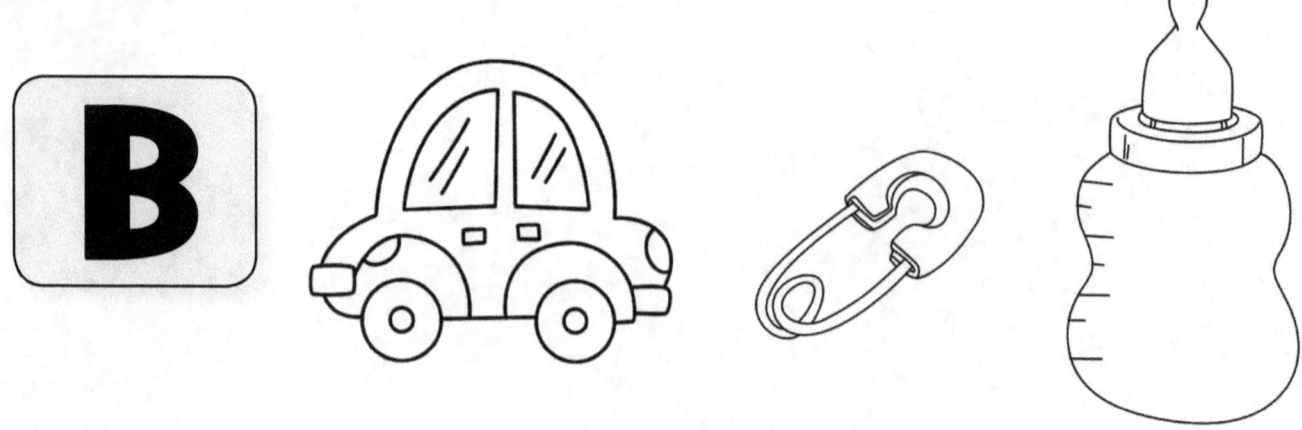

What shape comes next?

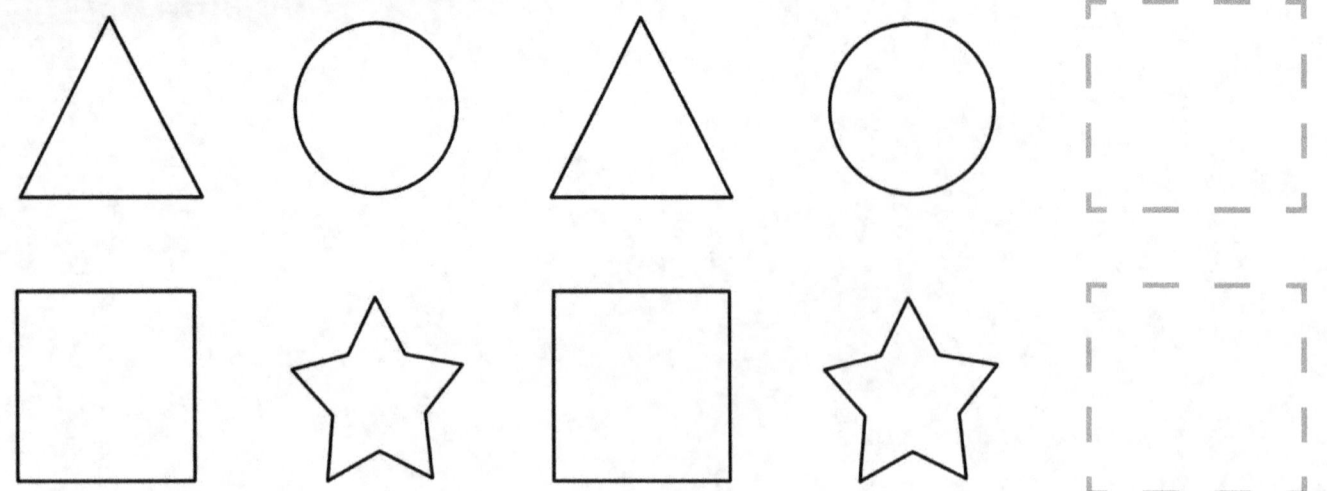

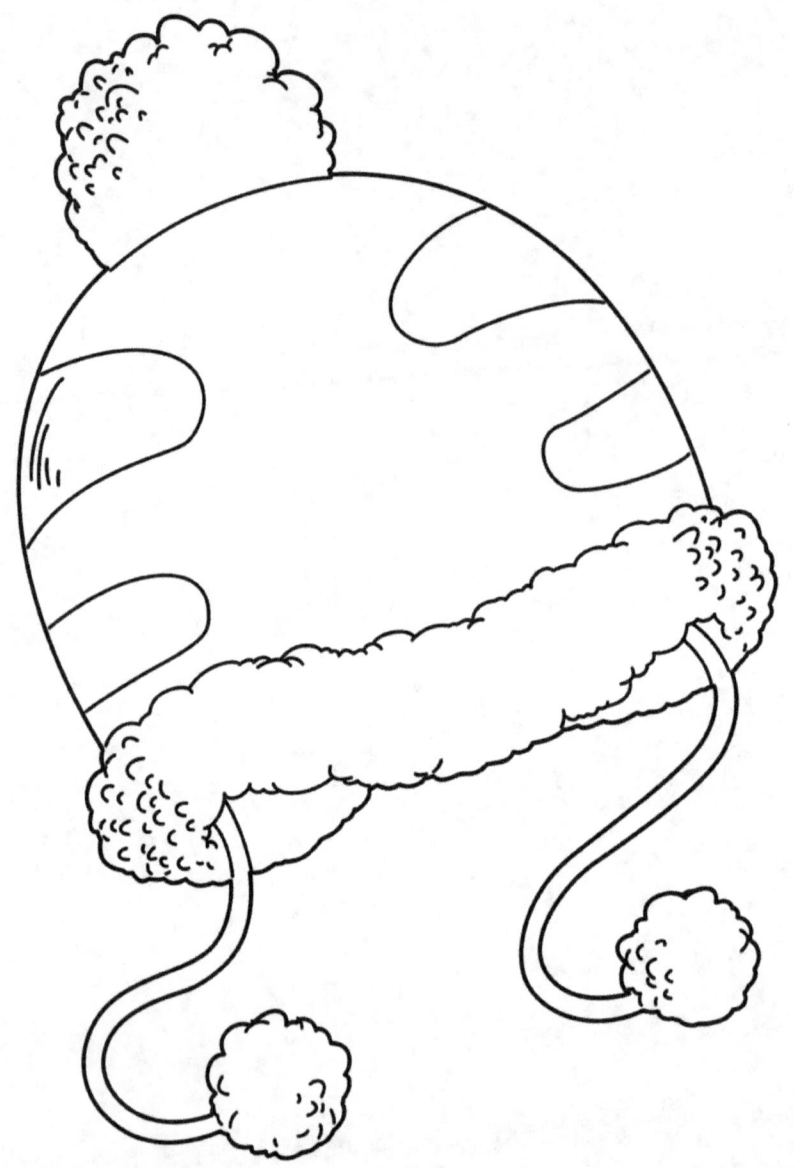

How many?

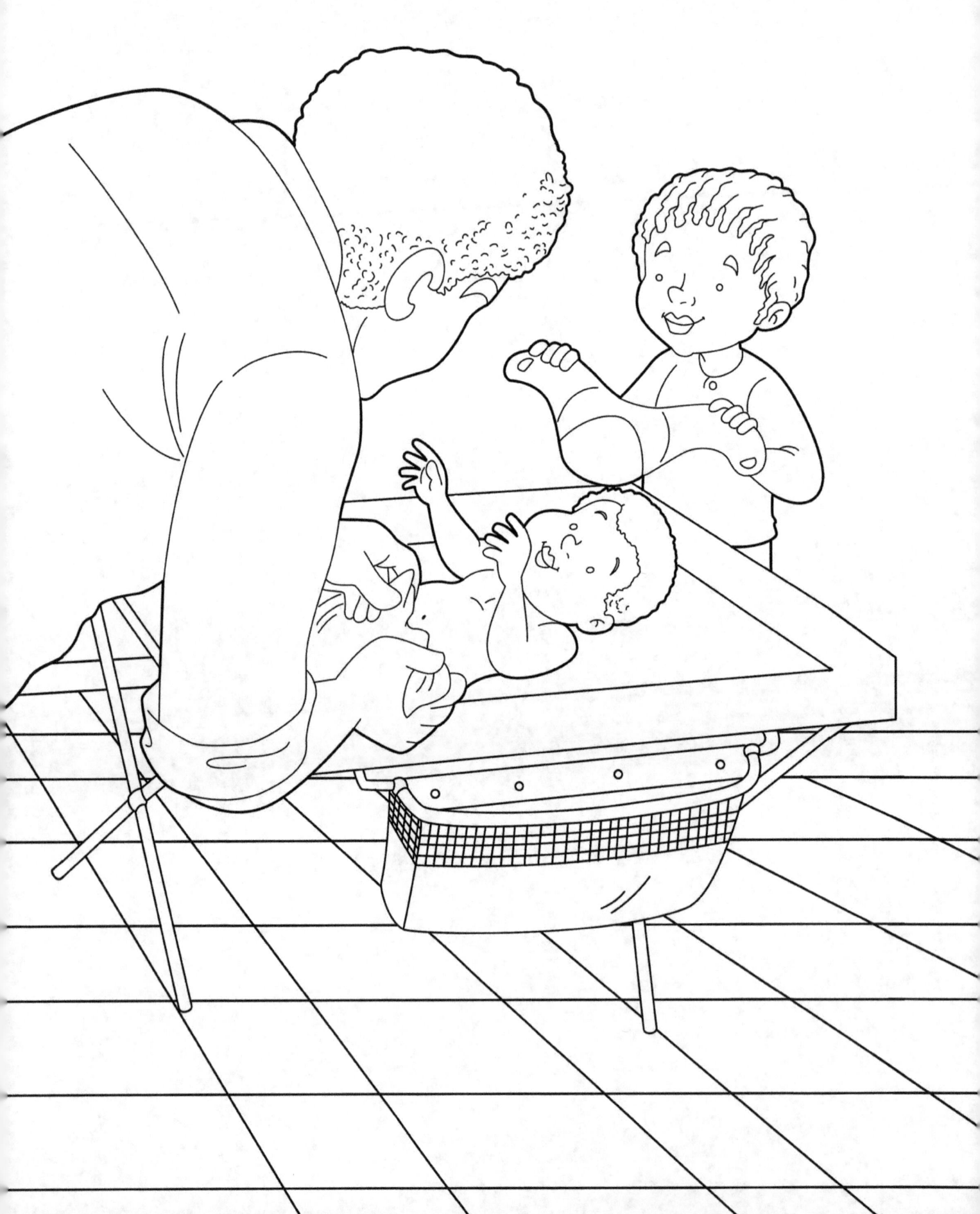

Trace the line to help baby reach the toy.

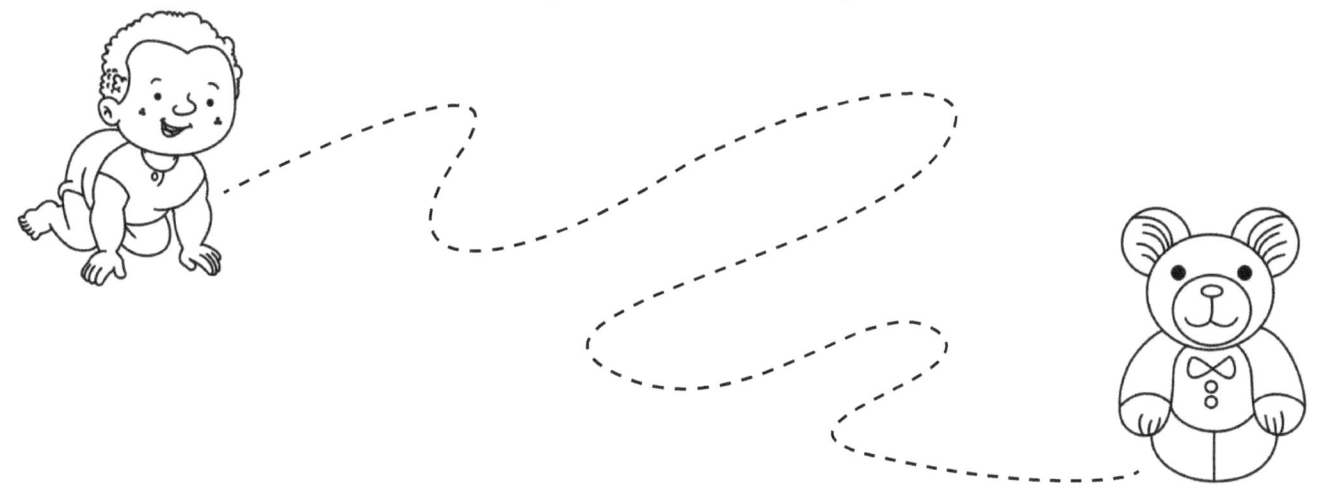

Find 3 differences in the two given pictures.

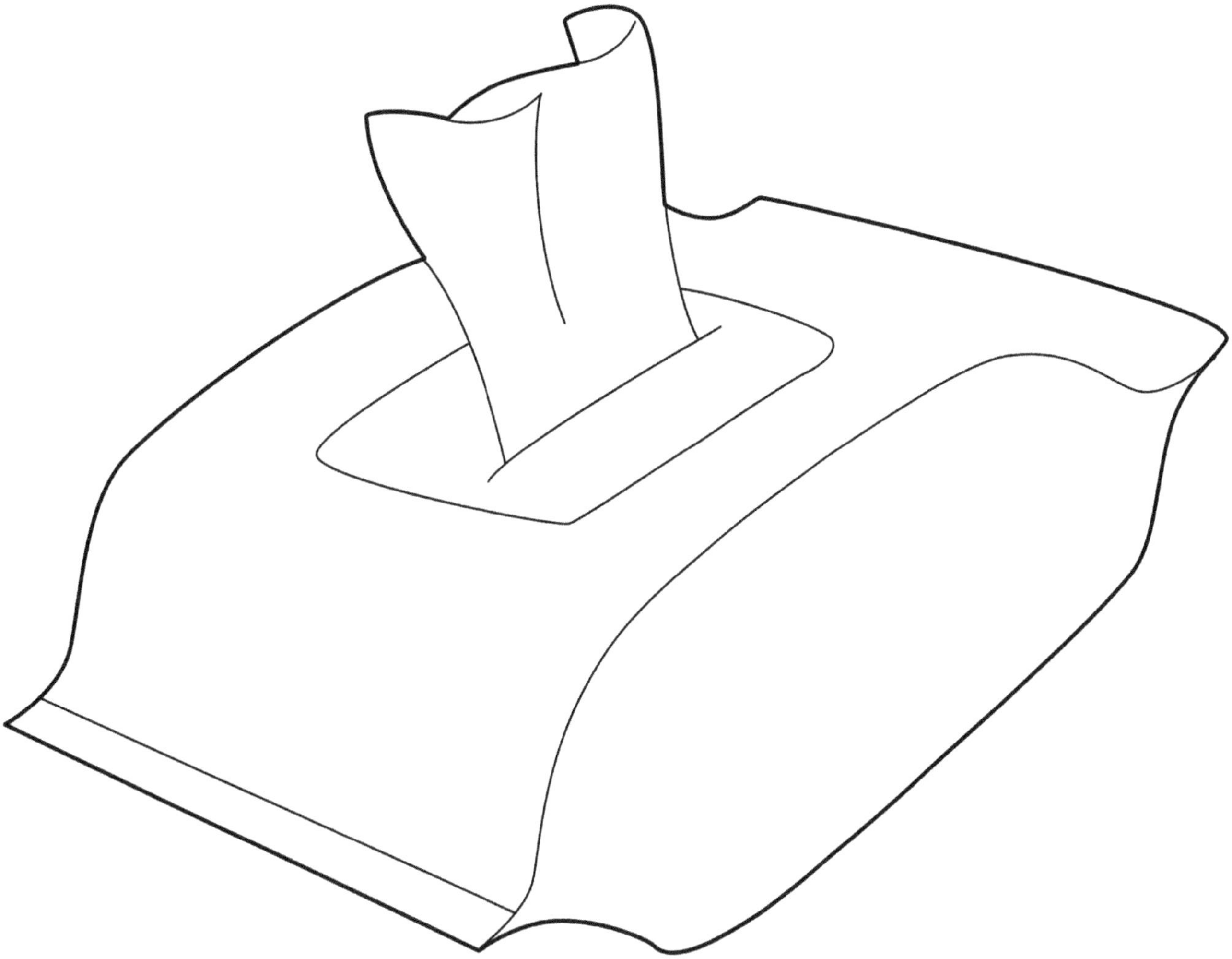

Find the two same pictures.

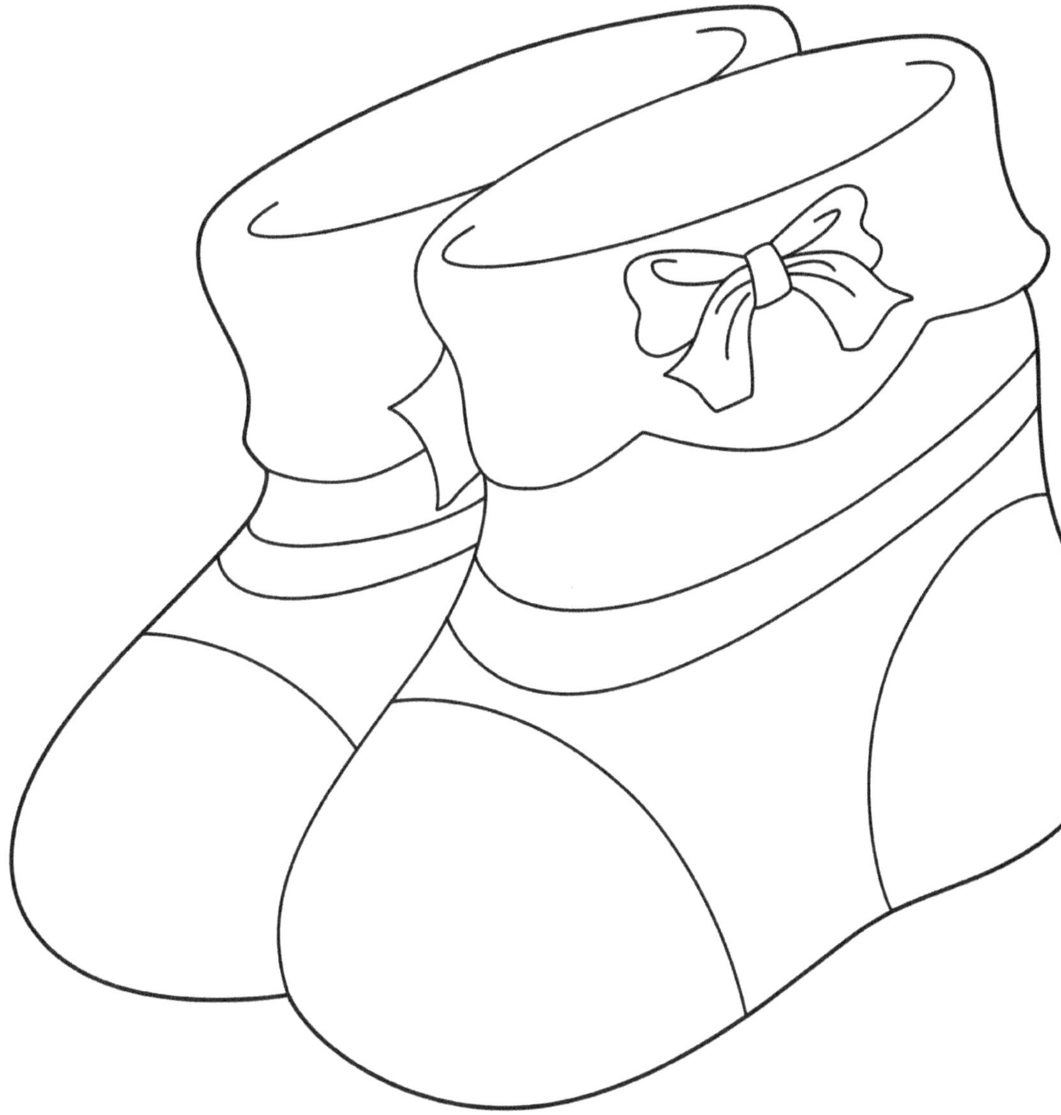

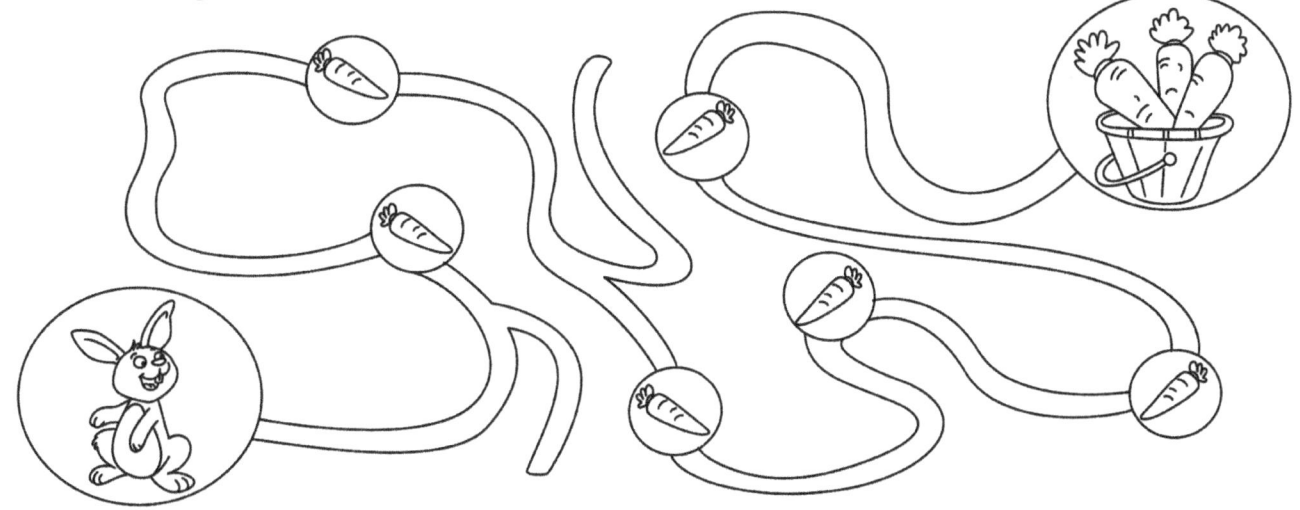

Help bunny to reach the pail of carrots.

How many of each are there.

Spell the word.

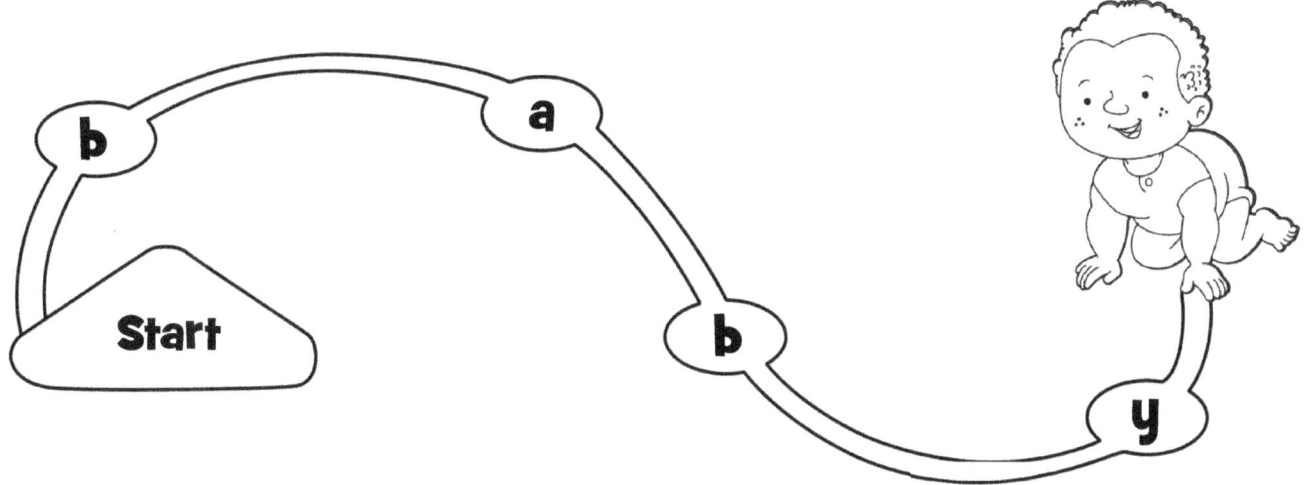

Start · b · a · b · y

Circle the one that is Smallest.

Handwriting practice.

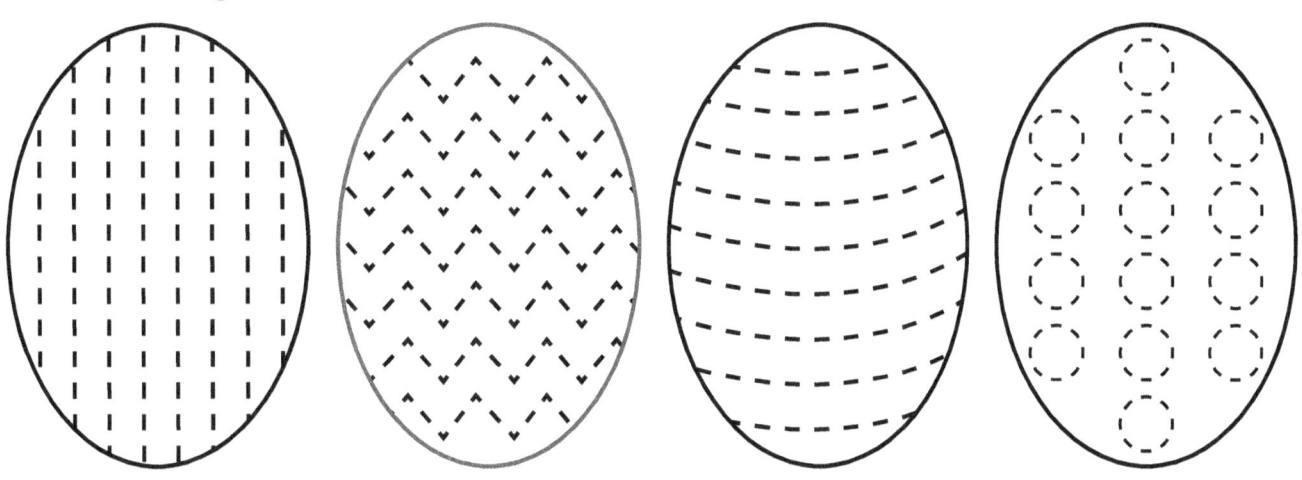

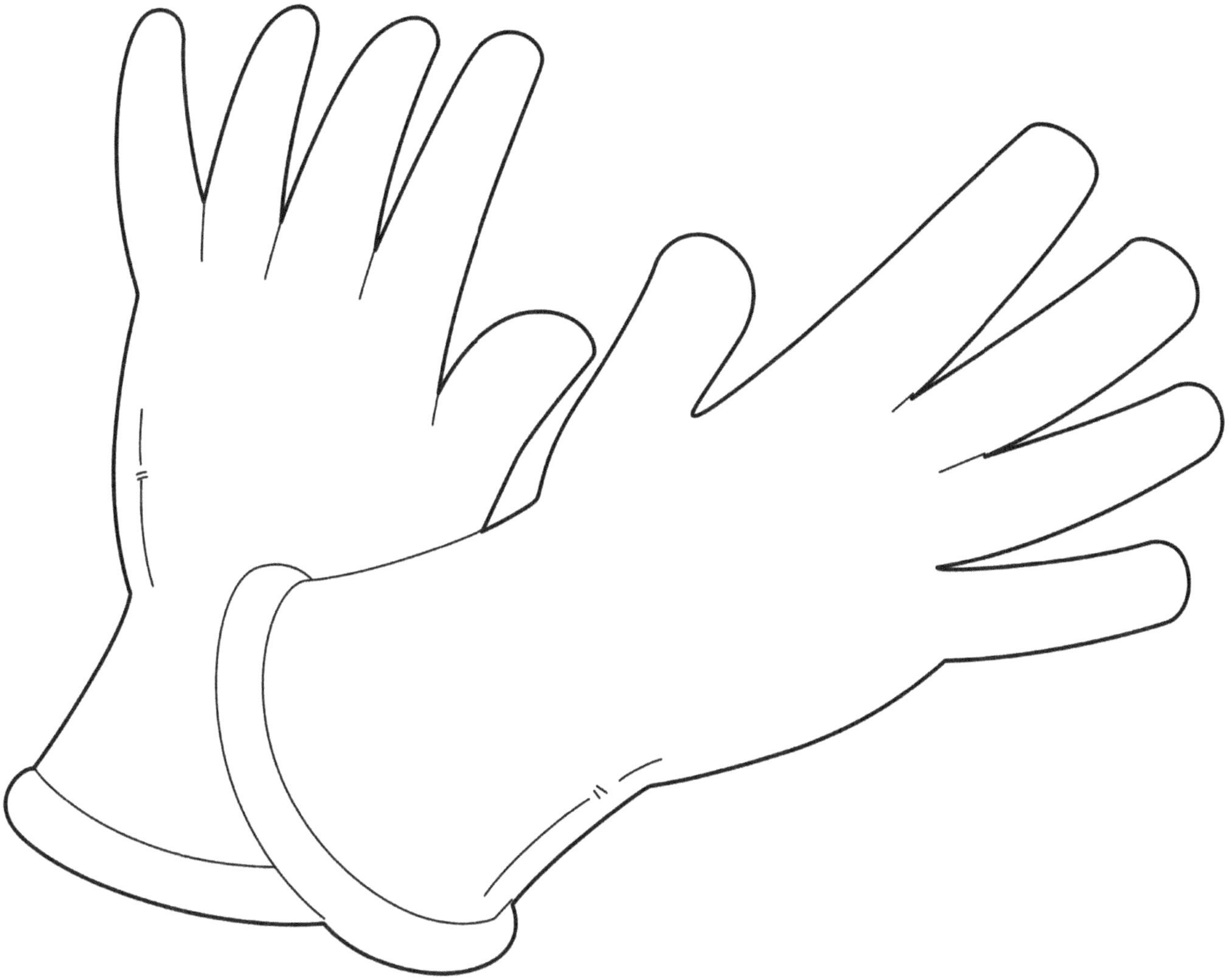

What comes next?

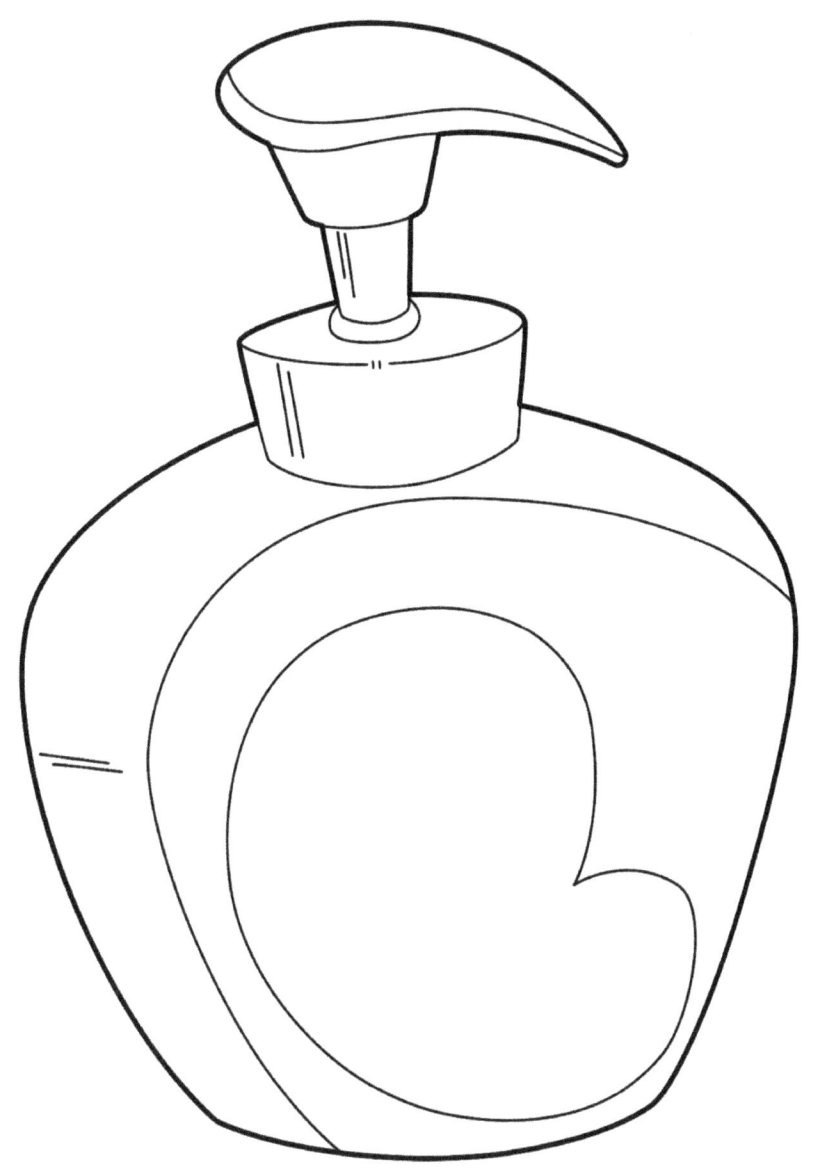

Help babies find their way.

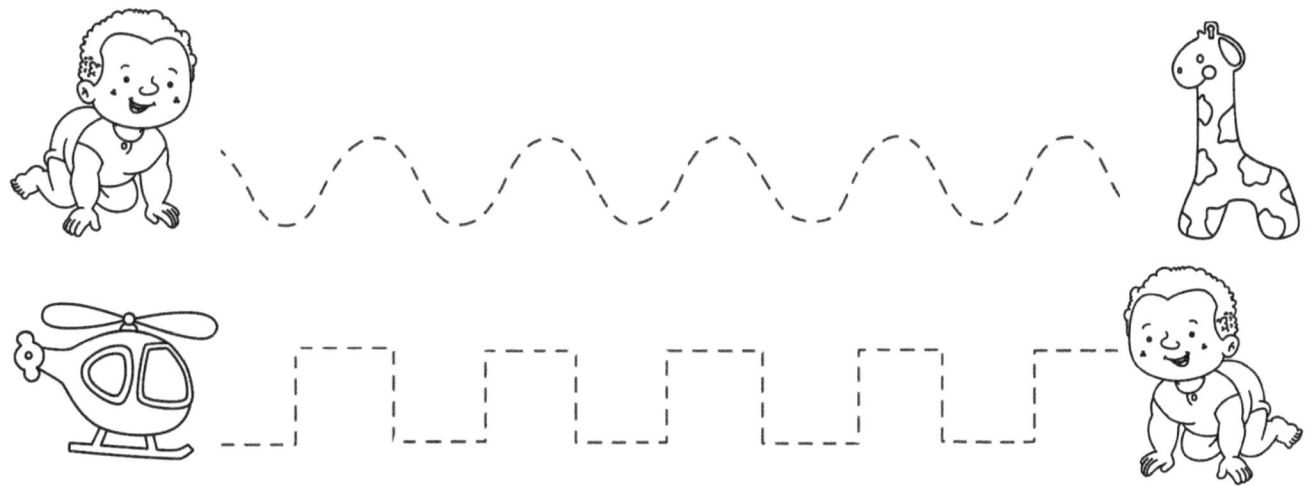

Words Puzzle.

S

L

E T

O L

R

R

⬜ ⬜ ⬜ ⬜ ⬜ ⬜ ⬜ ⬜

Complete each picture by drawing the other half.

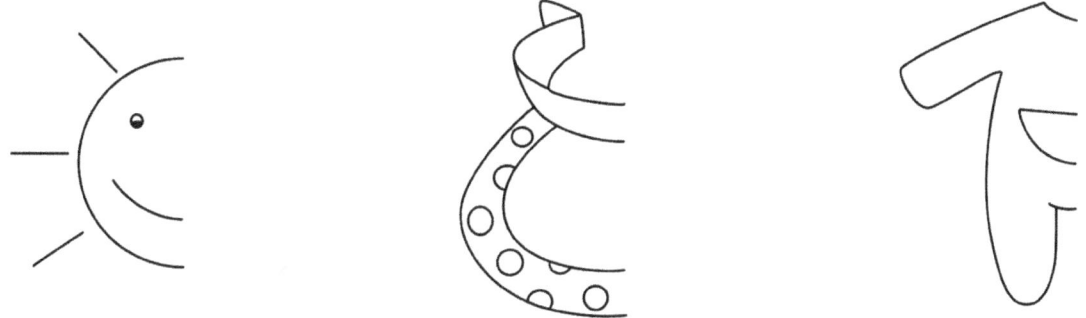

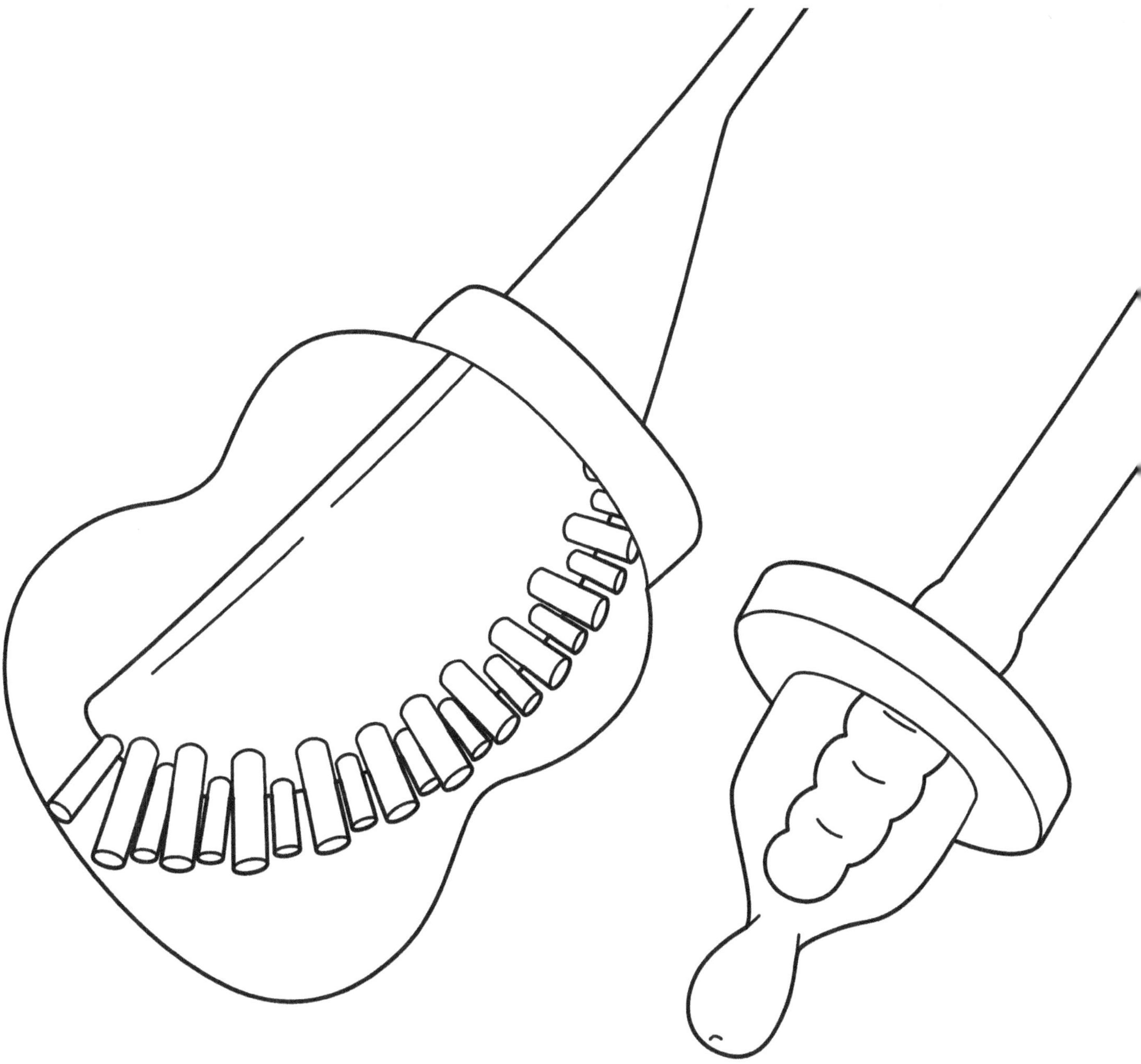

Connect the dots.

Match the picture with the alphabet.

D

P

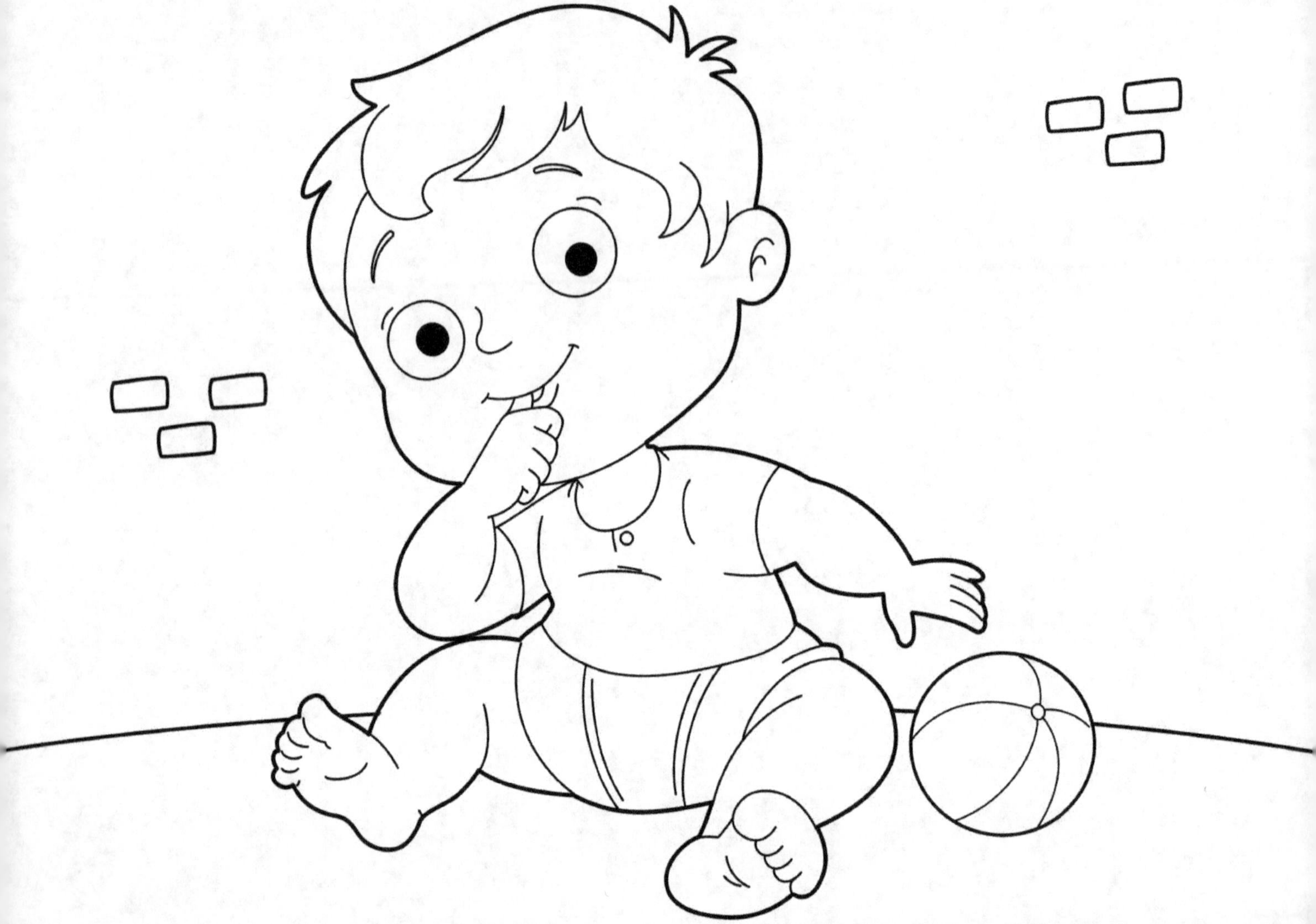

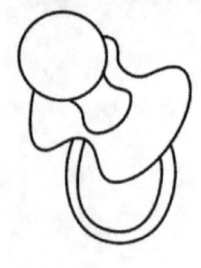

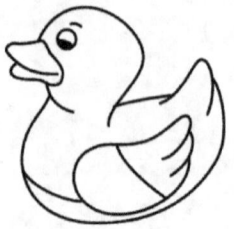

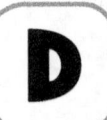

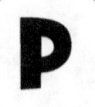

Circle the biggest object.

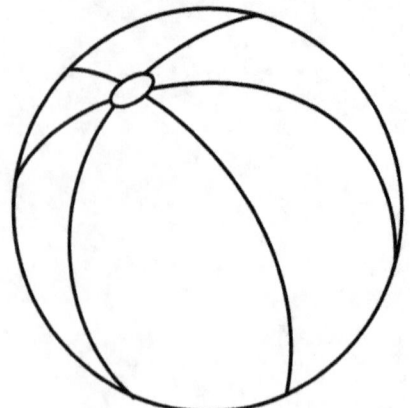  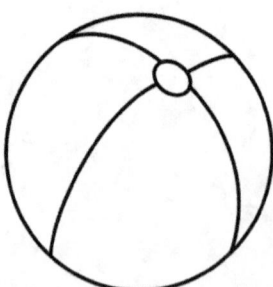

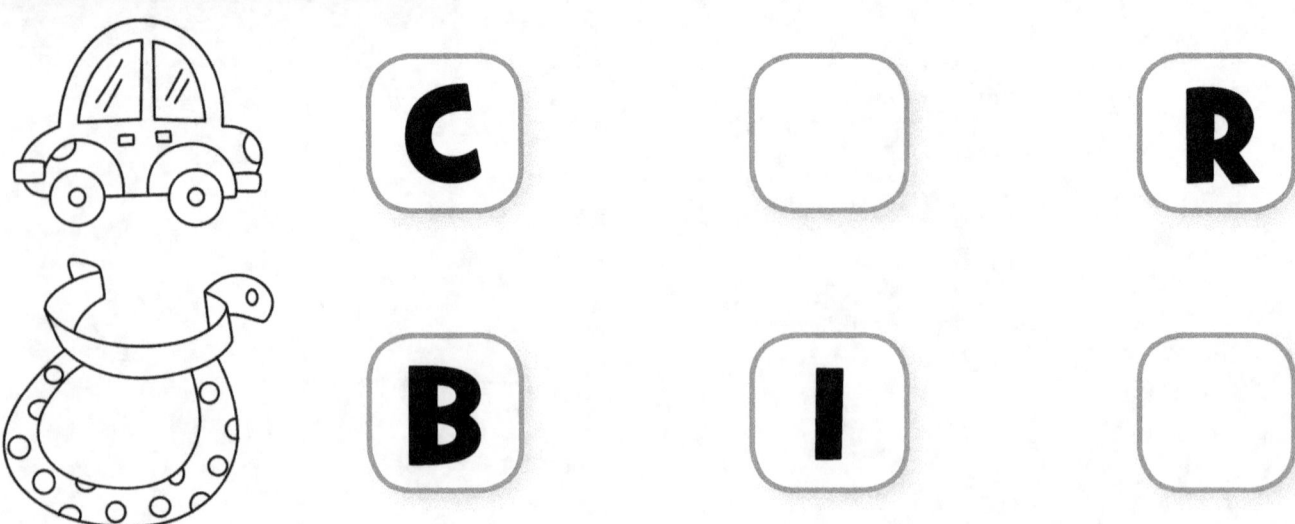

Write the missing letter.

C   [ ]   R

B   I   [ ]

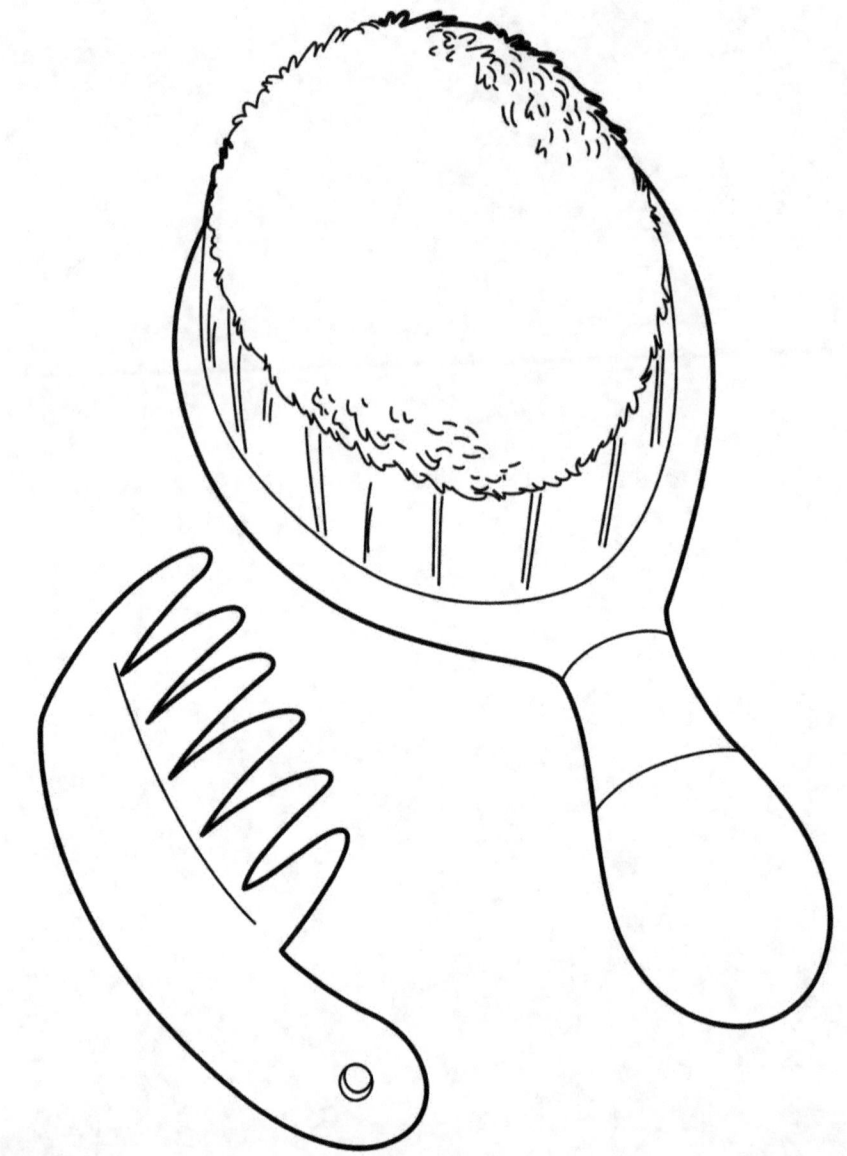

Join the dots from 1 - 10.

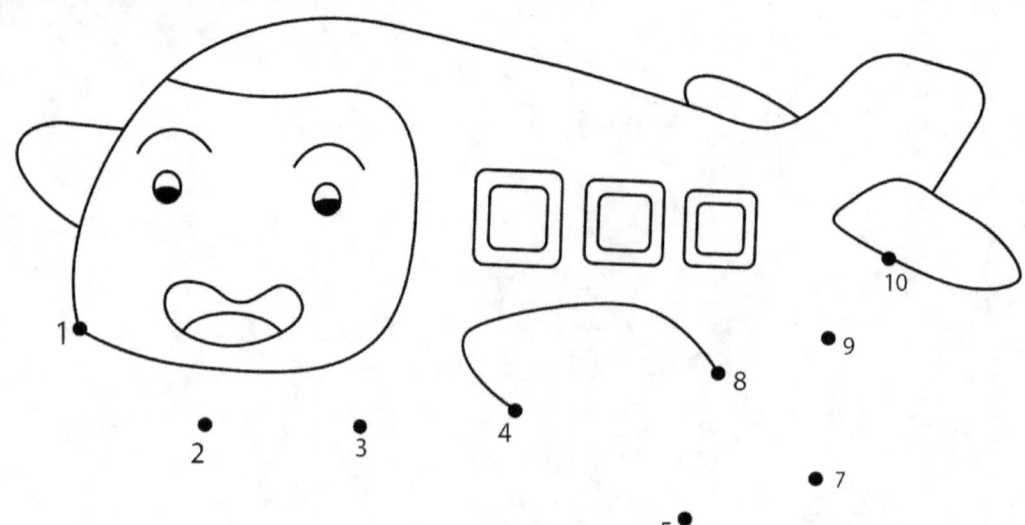

1

2

3

4

5

6

7

8

9

10

Love this book or any other by Author Marcia 'Cia' Harris?

We would appreciate your gift of a ** review on Amazon

*** Please like and Share with you family and friends

***Please leave your comment on FB and Tag us

FB: rhymingwithmarcia

Email: Dreams_2reality@outlook.com

Social media links

Facebook: https://www.facebook.com/marcia.harris.3386

TikTok: www.tiktok.com/@marcia_cia_harris

Instagram: https://www.instagram.com/rhymingwithmarcia/

Twitter: https://twitter.com/MarciaCiaHarri1

***Invite us to share your Kiddies functions and parties